"Let's all play hide and seek. It's a good game," said Ash to Eddy. "Can Scrap and Scully play with us too?" Eddy asked.

"Ok. Your turn first," said Ash. "You and Scrap hide and we will search for you."

Eddy and Scrap ran off to look for a good place to hide.

They hid in a dark place.
"Stay under here, Scrap. We
mustn't say or bark a word!"
Eddy said.

"Five, four, three, two, one … here we come!" called Ash.

"Let's search in the hall first. You look under that heap of coats!" Ash said.

"Come on Scully,
let's take a peek
here," said Ash.

"No. Not here!" thought Scully.

Don't wag your tail, Scrap.

"I bet they are in here.
Let's creep up on them!"
said Ash.

"No. Not here!"
thought Scully.

Don't even
peep out,
Scrap!

"Where did they sneak off to?
I give up!" Ash said.

"We need to look upstairs," thought Scully.

Ash and Scully
went upstairs.
They went into
Eddy's bedroom.

They heard a sneeze
from under the bed!

"What a relief! Our turn now." thought Scully.

Puzzle Time

Match the words to the picture if they have the same sound in them. One has been done for you.

Look out! They may be different spellings for the same sound.

thought

sn<u>ee</u>ze

b<u>ir</u>d

funny

draw

turn

t<u>ai</u>l

game

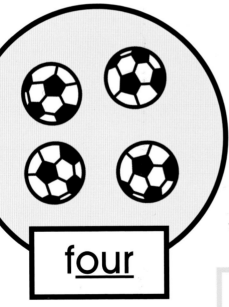

search

stay

f<u>our</u>

sneak

Answers

sneeze – funny is already completed to show how the same sound but different letters can make a pair.

sneeze /ee/ – sneak

tail /ai/ – game, stay

bird /ur/ – search, turn

four /or/ – draw, thought

A note about the phonics in this book

Alternative spellings of known phonemes

Known phonemes	New graphemes/spellings	Words in the story
/ee/	ea, e-e, ie, y	seek, three, heap, hear, peek, creep, even, peep, sneak, need, sneeze, relief
/ur/	ear, or, ir	turn, search, word, first, heard
/ai/	ay, a-e	play, game, stay, say, place, tail
/or/	our, augh, ough	four, your, thought, caught
common words	here	
tricky common words	asked, called	

Remind children about the letters they already know for these phonemes.

In the puzzle they are challenged to match the words to the picture if they have the same sound in them; the same sound but different letters.

Top tip: if a child gets stuck on a word then ask them to try and sound it out and then blend it together again or show them how to do this. For example, first, f-ir-s-t, first.